Fortune's Fool

Stacie Withers

Series Editor: John McRae

Thomas Nelson and Sons Ltd
Nelson House   Mayfield Road
Walton-on-Thames   Surrey
KT12 5PL   UK

51 York Place
Edinburgh
EH1 3JD   UK

Thomas Nelson (Hong Kong) Ltd
Toppan Building 10/F
22A Westlands Road
Quarry Bay   Hong Kong

First published by Edward Arnold, a division of Hodder and
Stoughton Ltd 1990

ISBN 0-340-52422-7

This edition first published by Thomas Nelson and Sons Ltd 1992

ISBN 0-17-556119-2
NPN 9 8 7 6 5 4 3 2

Printed in Hong Kong.

Chapter 1

It is early one Monday morning, but the fairground is already busy. Today is a public holiday in August and the weather is hot. The big wheel is turning round and you can see people in the little boxes high up in the sky. Children are riding the horses on the merry-go-round. Some older boys are trying to win coconuts. They are throwing balls at the coconuts and trying to knock them down. People are eating ice-creams or apples on sticks. An old man is selling big red balloons.

Madam Marenka is in her tent. She is a gipsy. She is wearing a long red dress and she has a red scarf over her hair. Her hair is long and black and her eyes are black too. She is wearing gold jewellery – big gold earrings in her ears and big gold bracelets on her arms. But the gold is not real gold because Madam Marenka is not very rich. People think that Madam Marenka sees the future. There is a big crystal ball on the table. Sometimes she looks into the crystal ball; sometimes she looks at people's hands and reads the future there; sometimes she reads the cards or even the tea leaves.

Marenka is not English, but she has lived in England all her life. Her parents came to England when she was a baby. They came from Hungary. They travelled slowly by road in their old gipsy wagon, with their big family of ten children. They had three sons and seven daughters. Marenka was the youngest. Marenka was very proud of

her parents. They were true gipsies, real gipsy people. Marenka's father was the gipsy king.

But now there are very few real gipsies. When Marenka's father was the gipsy king, there were many gipsies living in the fields and woods and countryside. There was singing and dancing, and they told old stories by the firelight. But everything has changed since then. Now all the gipsies have gone to live in the big towns and the groups of true gipsies in the countryside are very small. Even Marenka's brothers and sisters went to live in the towns; they took jobs and married there. They did not marry true gipsies and they forgot the old gipsy ways. This broke Marenka's father's heart. He was very sad when his children did not want to live like gipsies any more.

'We want a comfortable, modern way of life,' they said. 'We do not want to live in the woods and fields.' And they laughed at their father, the old gipsy king.

So they all left the gipsy camp, all except Marenka and her brother, Michael. Marenka's mother died when Marenka was ten years old and Marenka and Michael stayed with their old father. Marenka's father loved her very much because she was the child of his old age and because she had the same dark eyes and long black hair as her mother. When she was a little girl, Marenka often sat on her father's knee and he spoke to her in the strange language of the gipsies.

'Little Marenka, you are my seventh daughter. All the others have forgotten the gipsy ways. Be a true gipsy, my dear. Remember the gipsy ways and be true to them.'

Another time, her father said, 'Little Marenka, you are a true gipsy. You must always be free and proud. Never beg, never ask for money in the streets. You must work for your own money, or always be poor, but free.'

Marenka's father died when she was eighteen, but she did not marry like all her sisters. Marenka wanted to marry only a true gipsy, someone like her father, but there were very few true gipsies left. She did not want to live and work in a big town. So she and her brother, Michael, stayed together in the old Hungarian gipsy wagon. Michael now looks after horses – sometimes he even sells them; Marenka tells fortunes at the fairground. They do not make a lot of money, but they are comfortable and happy. They are free and proud, like their father.

Chapter 2

So Marenka is happy on this hot Monday morning holiday in August. It is a busy day and perhaps she will make some money. She enjoys working in the fairground because she likes meeting people. Marenka's mother taught her to tell fortunes when she was a little girl. But Marenka cannot really see the future; she just pretends.

'I have no special magic powers because I am a gipsy,' she says to herself. 'People believe a lot of nonsense! Of course I can't really see the future. But people *think* I can and this makes them happy.'

Marenka always tells people good things. She likes seeing people happy. When people are happy, they also pay her well.

'Here comes my first client of the day!' thinks Marenka, as a little old lady comes into the tent. The old lady is wearing a black dress and a black hat. She looks very sad.

'This will be easy!' thinks Marenka. 'Someone in her family is probably dead. Her husband, perhaps?'

'Please sit down,' says Marenka.

'Thank you,' answers the old lady. 'This is my first visit to a fortune-teller. I'm very nervous. You see, my Joseph . . .'

'Don't be afraid,' says Marenka. 'Let me look into my crystal ball. Ah, I can see the picture of a young man and a young woman together! Now the picture darkens, and

they are growing older, older, older. Now I see the woman alone. Tell me, have you lost your husband recently, my dear?'

'Yes, yes,' says the old lady. 'My Joseph died six months ago, after nearly fifty years of marriage. How did you know?'

'My crystal ball tells me many things,' says Marenka. 'I am a medium. Now in my crystal, I can see an old man in the middle of some clouds. He is smiling. Your husband is happy in the afterlife, and he wants you to be happy. You will see him again one day.'

'Oh, that is wonderful,' says the old lady. 'Thank you so much. I so much wanted someone to talk to. My son gets very impatient with me. He tells me that it's time to forget the past and live in the present. But I can't forget.'

The old lady pays Marenka and goes out smiling.

'I make people happy simply because I tell them good things,' says Marenka to herself. 'It's easy.'

Almost immediately a young man comes in. He is wearing very expensive clothes, but they are flashy. His shirt is bright pink and he has an ugly tie. He is chewing gum.

'I only came in here for a joke,' he says. 'My friends are laughing like mad outside.'

Marenka looks into her crystal ball and tells him he is making a lot of money and that he will make more.

'But I also see a man dressed in blue,' Marenka adds with a smile. 'Perhaps you'd better be careful of the police.'

'You are probably right there!' answers the young man. He pays Marenka five pounds.

'It's a lot of money, but it's worth it for the laugh,' he says.

'I am having a very good day,' thinks Marenka. 'It is easy to make guesses about the lives of these people. I can make some money *and* make people happy. I only tell them things they know already.'

After lunch, a fat man comes in. He has a loud, jolly laugh. Marenka can smell beer on his breath. She tells him that he enjoys life; he likes eating and drinking with his friends.

'But be careful,' she says. 'I can also see a man in a white coat in my crystal ball. You'd better not eat and drink so much or you'll be ill.'

The man pays Marenka and leaves. He pays more attention to Marenka's advice than to his doctor's.

Marenka is really happy now. She is doing a useful job. People are listening to her and taking her advice. She is also making a lot of money today.

When Marenka gets home, she and her brother, Michael, always sit in the Hungarian gipsy wagon and drink tea together. Marenka makes different kinds of tea from herbs. Michael talks about the horses and Marenka tells him about her day at the fairground. Today, while they sip their tea, she is telling him about the visitors to her tent – the old lady, the flashy young man and the jolly fat man.

'They all believed me so easily,' she says. '*They* told me about their lives; the crystal didn't tell me. There was no magic in it.'

'What fools they are!' says Michael.

'Maybe. But they are happy fools,' answers Marenka.

'People will believe anything,' continues Michael. 'Take the tea, for example. You put herbs in it. These herbs cure our headaches or calm our nerves, and people say this is the magic of the gipsies. But there is no magic; Mother simply taught you to get the right herbs when you were a child.'

'And the flowers when Father died!' exclaims Marenka. 'Do you remember? After Father died, I put flowers on his grave every week. I always went to his grave at night-time because I wanted to be alone. No one ever saw me. And because no one ever saw me, people thought that the flowers arrived every week by magic. You are right, Michael. People *are* fools!'

'Except the gipsies, Marenka. The gipsies are not fools!' Michael laughs and adds, 'We clever gipsies can take the money from the fools.'

'But Michael,' says Marenka seriously, 'there are so few true gipsies left.'

Chapter 3

The next morning, Tuesday, Marenka arrives at her tent at 8.30. A pretty young girl with long blond hair is already standing outside the tent. Marenka is surprised to see anyone there so early.

'I'm sorry to trouble you,' says the girl, 'but can you really tell fortunes and see the future? I very much want some advice.'

The girl looks up at Marenka with big, unhappy blue eyes. Marenka studies the girl's worried face.

'You'd better come in and sit down,' says Marenka.

The girl is a little shy, but she goes into the tent.

'My grandmother told me to come,' says the girl. 'Grannie came to see you yesterday. She says that you can see the future. She says you are very clever.'

Marenka remembers the little old lady in black and smiles.

'I can talk to Grannie,' continues the girl, 'but I can't talk to my mother and father. That's why I came here early today – my parents don't know I'm with a fortune-teller. If they learn I'm here, my mother will laugh and my father will get angry. Grannie is the only person who listens.'

The girl sits down and puts her hands on the table. Marenka notices a sparkling diamond ring on the fourth finger of the girl's left hand.

'I'll read your hand,' says Marenka.

Marenka takes the girl's hand. 'She is wearing an engagement ring,' thinks Marenka. 'I'll tell her that she will marry a handsome young man. They will be happy – and rich too, if he can buy her diamonds like that! Perhaps there is a silly little reason why she is unhappy. Perhaps a silly quarrel with her young man? But soon she will be happy again. I'll say something nice.'

Marenka opens her mouth to speak, but suddenly she feels a terrible pain in her head. There is a singing noise in her ears. Inside her head, she hears a voice saying, 'Death! Death! Death!'

What can this mean? Can Marenka really know the future after all? This is the first time she has heard a voice like this. It is a real voice too. Marenka is not pretending.

Marenka puts her hands to her head. Her face is white. She hears the sweet but nervous voice of the girl. The girl is asking, 'Are you all right? What's the matter?'

Will the girl die? Will her young man die? How can Marenka tell the girl that the future means death?

Marenka hears the voice again, 'Death! Death! Death!' but this time the voice is not so strong.

'I must control myself,' thinks Marenka. 'I have worked very hard recently and the weather has been hot. I am probably a little ill. I am making a mistake. There is no real voice – it is not possible.'

Marenka looks at the girl again. Marenka speaks slowly and clearly.

'You will marry a rich, handsome young man,' she says. 'But there is a small problem with your family. Now

I shall look into my crystal.' Marenka is calm now. Her crystal ball is cloudy.

'Good,' thinks Marenka. 'It was only my imagination.'

Then, in the crystal, a strange shape slowly appears. This is the first time Marenka has seen anything in her crystal ball; she has always pretended before. Now Marenka sees an ugly, white skull with long hair down to the shoulders. She is frightened.

'The Death's Head,' she says to herself in alarm.

Marenka looks at the girl, who has long blond hair down to her shoulders, and then she looks at the ugly skull with long hair like old string. She is full of fear and horror. How can she tell the girl what she can see? Of course she cannot. She must lie. In a weak voice, Marenka says.

'You will marry. You will have children, but I can see an angry man in my crystal. Perhaps it is your father?'

'That's right,' says the girl. 'Daddy doesn't want me to marry Paul, but Mummy . . . '

'Lucky guess,' thinks Marenka. Then she continues, 'I can see a woman in my crystal too. She is smiling at the young man. Perhaps the woman is your mother?'

'Yes, but Mummy only wants me to marry Paul because he is rich,' says the girl. 'She and Daddy quarrel all the time about it. I am very unhappy.'

'What do *you* want to do, my dear?'

'Oh, I love Paul. I want to marry him. He is a very exciting person. He's very strong and he's never afraid of anything. Not a bit like me!'

'Then you will marry him,' says Marenka. 'Don't worry. Everything will be all right. Your father will accept

14

him in the end.'

'Thank you so much,' says the girl. 'Grannie was right. You are very clever. Now, how much money do I pay you?'

'Nothing, my dear,' answers Marenka. 'My first client of the day brings me good luck – but only if the client doesn't pay. Today you are my first client.'

'Oh, but I must pay something,' the girl says and leaves some money on the table.

'I wish you good luck in the future,' Marenka says, as the girl leaves. Marenka is now very unhappy. Is she really a medium after all? Can she really see the future? She really did see a skull in her crystal ball; she did not pretend. Does the skull mean death? Is the girl's future so black?

Marenka writes 'CLOSED' in big letters on a piece of paper. She puts the 'CLOSED' sign on the door of the tent. Then she sits down, puts her head in her hands and tries to think.

Chapter 4

That evening, Marenka sits in the gipsy wagon and waits for her brother Michael to come home. She drinks her tea and looks at the lamplight on the rich red carpet. The carpet is old but beautiful and its colours are still rich. It covers not only the floor, but also the walls and ceiling; this keeps the wagon warm in winter. But now, in August, it is very hot inside the wagon. Marenka cannot relax. She does not feel calm tonight.

At last, she hears Michael's footsteps. He gives a low whistle, as usual, as he comes near, and Wildfire and Storm, their two horses, answer with a welcoming 'neigh'. Michael comes into the wagon. He immediately sees that something is wrong.

'What's the matter?' he asks his sister.

Marenka tells him everything about the girl, about the voice inside her head and the skull that appeared in the crystal ball.

Michael listens carefully. He does not laugh. When Marenka has finished her story, he says. 'You know, Marenka, perhaps you can see the future, after all.'

'Nonsense,' replies Marenka. 'How can anyone see the future? It's impossible.'

'*We* always say it is nonsense,' says Michael. 'But Mother didn't think so. She believed it. And after all, you are a seventh daughter and you are always proud that you are a true gipsy.'

17

'Then do you think that true gipsies really can see the future, Michael?'

'I don't know,' answers her brother. 'But how else can we explain the voice inside your head? And what about the skull in the crystal ball? What does that mean?'

'What shall we do? Is that pretty girl going to die?' asks Marenka.

'I have an idea,' says Michael. 'Do you remember Mother's special tarot cards?'

'Yes, of course,' answers Marenka. 'Those tarot cards have been with Mother's family for more than two hundred years, always passed from mother to daughter. Our grandmother gave them to mother and, before that, our great-grandmother owned them. I never take them to the fairground – they are much too precious.'

'Well, Marenka, I think you'd better get Mother's tarot cards now and read them,' advises Michael. 'They are special cards and this is a special problem.'

So Marenka goes to the cupboard and takes out her mother's pack of tarot cards. The cards are old, but they are very beautiful because each card is hand painted. Marenka carefully lays four cards in a circle and puts one card in the middle. The fifth card shows a picture of two lovers. The lovers are looking at each other.

'The Lovers!' exclaims Michael. 'Of course – that must mean the pretty girl at the fairground with her young man? But are the lovers on the card staying together? Or are they saying goodbye?'

'Ssh, Michael,' answers Marenka. 'I must lay out one more card.'

Marenka takes a sixth card from the pack and lays it on top of the Lovers. The sixth card shows a picture of a large wheel.

'The Wheel of Fortune!' exclaims Marenka. 'So there will be a change of fortune for the lovers. That pretty girl and her young man are happily in love now; perhaps that will soon change. Or perhaps the girl's parents will change their ideas about him?'

'Well, Marenka,' says Michael. 'You cannot help them. Fortune will take its own course. Now,' he advises, 'I think you'd better get some sleep. Tomorrow will be another busy day for you at the fairground.'

Chapter 5

The next morning, Wednesday, Marenka is in her tent again.

'Will that pretty girl come back today?' she wonders.

Marenka spends the whole day in her tent, but the girl does not come back. In the early evening, Marenka decides to go home. She makes her way through the crowded fairground. There are a lot of people there because it is a warm summer evening.

Suddenly, Marenka sees the girl with a tall, young man. They are standing near the big wheel.

'So that is Paul!' thinks Marenka. 'He is certainly very good-looking.' Then suddenly Marenka remembers the tarot cards.

'The Wheel of Fortune in the cards!' she exclaims aloud. 'Good heavens! The picture is exactly like the big wheel at the fairground! And the lovers are standing next to it, just as those two cards were next to each other in the pack!'

Then, as she looks at the young couple, Marenka suddenly feels a sharp pain in her head. She hears the same voice as yesterday. The voice comes from inside her head and slowly repeats the words. 'Death! Death! Death!'

'The big wheel!' she exclaims. 'Is it dangerous? Will there be an accident?'

Marenka quickly makes her way over to the big wheel. As she comes near, she hears Paul's voice.

'Oh, come on, Julia,' he is saying. 'It'll be exciting up there. Don't be afraid. I'll look after you. It's not dangerous.'

Marenka sees Paul buy the tickets. The girl looks very nervous. Marenka suddenly screams out.

'Don't go near that big wheel! Please don't go near it!'

Paul only turns round and laughs. But the ticket-seller isn't laughing.

'Clear off, you!' shouts the ticket-seller to Marenka. 'Are you crazy?'

'Why, it's the gipsy fortune-teller!' the girl exclaims in surprise. Then she and Paul get into their seats.

'Be careful, miss,' says the ticket-seller. 'Mind your hair. It's very long. You don't want to catch that lovely blond hair of yours in the mechanism of the wheel, do you?'

Marenka watches. She is afraid, very afraid indeed. What will happen to the girl? The big wheel starts to turn slowly. Then it goes faster, round and round. Marenka can see the girl's long blond hair. Her hair is flying out in the wind because she is high up at the top of the big wheel. The big wheel stops for two minutes and some more people get on. Those two minutes pass very slowly. Marenka holds her breath. Then the big wheel turns and comes down again. Paul and the girl get off. The girl is a little white, but she is laughing now. Paul has his arm round her. They are safe. They walk away from the big wheel.

'I am probably just an imaginative fool,' thinks Marenka, 'but I still want to follow them. I must find a way to warn that girl and save her. But save her from what? I don't know. But I just cannot forget the skull in my crystal ball and the voice inside my head, saying 'Death! Death! Death!'

Chapter 6

Paul and the girl go out of the gates of the fairground. Marenka follows them. They get into a red sports car and drive off. Then Marenka sees a taxi.

'What a stroke of luck!' she thinks.

The taxi driver is surprised when he sees the gipsy, but he stops. 'Can you pay?' he asks. 'Gipsies don't usually take taxis.'

'Yes, yes, I'll pay anything. Only please follow that car,' Marenka says, as she jumps into the taxi. Paul's car is in the distance. He is driving fast.

'Faster, faster, please!' says Marenka to the taxi driver. 'I'll give you twice the money.'

Marenka has a five-pound note. The flashy young man in the bright pink shirt gave it to her yesterday. She shows the five-pound note to the driver. She also shows him her bag of silver coins. The taxi driver goes very fast and soon they see Paul's car at the traffic lights. They follow Paul's car for thirty minutes. At last, the sports car stops outside a splendid house. The girl is getting out of the sports car just as the taxi comes round the corner.

'Good-bye, Julia. I'll take you to the seaside on Saturday! We'll go to Whitecliff Sands again!' Paul calls out as he drives off. Julia waves good-bye to Paul and goes into the house.

'Well, I know the girl's name is Julia,' thinks Marenka. 'Lucky girl! Whitecliff Sands is a very nice place.'

'That's fifteen quid,' says the taxi driver to Marenka.

'Fifteen pounds!' exclaims Marenka. 'That's a lot of money.'

'Well, you said twice the money and I drove very fast. I nearly had an accident, didn't I? It's a good thing there were no policemen about.'

'All right, then,' says Marenka. She gives him the five-pound note and counts ten pounds of silver coins.

'What! All that small change too!' the taxi driver complains. 'That's just like the gipsies! They make the car dirty too!'

He drives off, complaining about gipsies under his breath. He leaves Marenka standing on the pavement. She is hurt and angry because the driver thinks that gipsies are dirty. She looks at the lovely house and thinks of the girl, Julia. She begins to feel envious.

'Perhaps it is not so good to be a gipsy, after all,' she thinks. 'That girl is rich, young, pretty and in love. What more could anyone want?'

And a voice inside her head answers, 'Life! Life! Life!'

Marenka waits outside the house. An hour passes. The sun is going down and she is feeling a little cold now. Then a man walks quickly down the street. He is about fifty years old. He is wearing a smart suit and he is carrying a newspaper. He looks like a successful businessman. He stops outside the house. He looks surprised, but not very pleased, when he sees Marenka there.

'This is probably Julia's father,' thinks Marenka. 'I must warn him. But will he listen to me? He is probably surprised to see a gipsy in the best part of town.'

Marenka approaches the man.

'Excuse me, sir . . . ' she begins.

'I have nothing for you, my good woman. I never give money to beggars,' he says immediately. 'Why don't you work for a living?'

'I am not a beggar, sir,' says Marenka quickly. 'I am proud to be a gipsy. I have never asked for anything in my life.'

'Well, I don't want to buy anything, either. No lucky white heather for me,' the man replies. 'I know what you gipsies are like. You don't work, that's your trouble.'

'I *do* work! I work very hard,' says Marenka. 'Please listen to me.'

'I said "No!" ' shouts the man angrily.

'It's about your daughter and Paul,' Marenka continues quickly. The man stops when he hears Paul's name.

'Well, what is it?' he says. 'Hurry up, I'm in a hurry.'

'You don't want her to marry Paul, do you, sir?' says Marenka.

'No, I don't. That reckless young man, with his dangerous driving and his flashy sports car. If he's not more careful, he'll get himself killed one day – or kill her – in that fast sports car of his. But I don't expect to discuss my private family affairs with a gipsy.'

Marenka hears him say 'or kill her in that fast sports car of his' and her heart beats faster. Was that what the voice meant by the words, 'Death! Death! Death!'? She tells him her story.

'Sir, I'm afraid your daughter is going to die. I want to

save her. I tell fortunes in the fairground. That is, I *pretend* to tell fortunes. I've never told a real fortune in my life. Not before yesterday! Your daughter came into my tent and I heard a voice saying "Death!" and I saw a skull in my crystal ball!'

Julia's father only gets more angry.

'Now just you listen to me!' he says. 'Why should I believe such rubbish? Rubbish, I say! It's your job to tell lies. You say so yourself. How many lies do you tell to all the people who come and see you in your tent? Someone has told you a lot about my family. If you think you can frighten me by saying you see death in your crystal ball, then you can think again!'

'But I'm telling the truth! I did see the death's head in my crystal!' answers Marenka. Now she is angry too.

'I don't believe you!' says Julia's father. 'I suppose money will make the picture of death disappear, eh? If I put silver in your palm, then you won't see death in your crystal any more and you'll tell me brighter things about the future. Perhaps my daughter didn't pay you enough! Well, you're not getting any money out of me! Now don't waste my time!'

With that, he turns and goes into the house.

Marenka for the first time in many years is crying. She is hurt and angry. She is tired and cold. She is also anxious about Julia.

'Poor Julia!' she thinks. 'She is rich, but she has an angry, impatient father and she will marry a selfish, spoilt young man. Her life isn't happy at all! That will teach me not to be envious of rich people!'

Chapter 7

In a beautiful dining-room with furniture of heavy wood, Julia and her parents are just finishing dinner. Julia has sat in silence through the dinner. She loves her father, but she does not talk to him very much because he is often angry and impatient. It is very difficult to please him; she always seems to do something wrong.

'You're very quiet tonight, Julia,' he says. 'Have you been out today?'

'Yes, I went to the fairground this afternoon.'

'The fairground! What a waste of time! Your grandmother was there the other day. I hope you didn't follow your grandmother's bad example and start talking to any gipsies!'

'But Daddy, Grannie said the gipsy fortune-teller helped her!'

The old woman who went to Marenka's tent was Julia's grandmother. Going to the fortune-teller helped her and comforted her. But now Julia and her father are quarrelling about the gipsy. He does not like gipsies, and says there was one outside the house, asking for money.

'A gipsy outside our house!' exclaims Julia's mother in horror.

'Yes, and I don't want Julia to speak to her. Do you hear, Julia? You must not talk to any gipsies in the street. These gipsies smile and say good things to your face but behind your back, they take your money and call you a fool! They bring you bad luck, not good.'

'All right, Daddy. I won't talk to any gipsies in the street,' promises Julia. 'They make me nervous.'

'Yes, you're a bag of nerves, just like your grandmother,' answers Julia's father. 'You didn't go to the fairground alone, did you?'

'No, Daddy. I went there with Paul.'

'Paul! But today is Wednesday. Why wasn't he at work?' asks Julia's father angrily.

'He didn't go to work this afternoon. He took the afternoon off,' answers Julia unhappily. She knows that her father will be very angry now, and there will be a quarrel.

'Lazy young man! We all know his uncle is rich and famous, but Paul should still work! You should study harder too! You must pass your exams this time!'

Julia feels really unhappy when her father says this. Last May she did very badly in her exams. She always studies hard, but she finds the work difficult. She is silent. She knows her father does not like Paul because he is rich.

'Paul!' exclaims Julia's father. 'He's so spoilt! He's had too much money, too young. And he has never had to work for it! He does not know the meaning of money – he will soon spend it all, and then he'll be poor. He spends every penny he can get his hands on.'

'Now it's not Paul's fault that he was born rich,' says Julia's mother. 'You are proud of your money too.'

'Yes, but I'm proud because I worked hard to make my money. Nobody gave it to me!' answers Julia's father angrily.

'Well, not everyone is like you,' says her mother.

Julia listens in nervous silence to her parents' quarrel. She thinks of Paul. She wants to get married to escape from the quarrels in her parents' house. She does not realise that Paul can be as angry and as difficult as her father.

Chapter 8

Meanwhile, Marenka has returned to a very different sort of home. It is hot inside the gipsy wagon, so she is standing outside it. There are a lot of stars tonight. Marenka breathes the fresh night air. She gives a piece of sugar to Storm, the old grey horse.

'What do you think, Storm?' she asks. 'Am I going mad or can I really see the future?'

Storm gives a friendly neigh. Marenka looks at the gipsy wagon. It is made of wood and beautifully carved. Because of the carving, it is not only beautiful but it is also light for the horse to pull.

'Ah, Storm,' she says. 'I am very proud of my beautiful home. Perhaps this gipsy wagon is more beautiful than Julia's house. But you are getting too old to pull even this wagon now. Poor Storm!'

Marenka leaves Storm and goes inside the wagon. She is feeling very sad tonight.

'Michael is late tonight,' she thinks. 'Where is he?' She wants to talk to her brother. She makes some herbal tea and sits down to wait.

'While I am waiting for Michael, I shall read the tarot cards again,' she says to herself. 'Yesterday I saw the card of the Lovers next to the Wheel and that proved true today. Perhaps I couldn't help Julia, but at least the cards told me the truth.'

So Marenka goes to the cupboard again and takes out

the beautiful pack of hand-painted tarot cards.

She lays out four cards in a circle. Then she puts a fifth card in the middle. The fifth card shows the picture of a man at the edge of a cliff. It is a long way down to the sea under the cliff. It is a long way to fall. The man is stepping over the edge of the cliff. Why is he stepping over the edge of the cliff? He is stepping into the unknown. It is a free fall. The name of this card is the Fool, or the Joker. This card has no number on it because it shows a step into the unknown.

'The Fool!' exclaims Marenka. 'This card has many meanings. Is the man a fool to step into the unknown? Or is he wise to step out, wise to trust the unknown future?'

Marenka then takes a sixth card from the pack. She lays it on top of the picture of the Fool. The sixth card shows the picture of a smiling skeleton on a horse.

'The Death card!' exclaims Marenka in horror. 'What does this mean? One card shows the Unknown and the next card shows Death! Perhaps we can never know how and when death will come. Are the cards saying that?'

Marenka puts the cards back in the cupboard and continues to wait for her brother to come home. At last she hears Michael's footsteps, his low whistle to the horses and their welcoming neigh. He comes into the wagon.

'Marenka!' he exclaims, when he sees her. 'You look so white and tired! Are you all right? Are you ill?'

Marenka tells him about the cards, the Fool and the Death card.

'You know, Marenka,' advises Michael. 'I think you should see a doctor. You are making yourself ill with worry.'

'A doctor?' questions Marenka, surprised. 'Let me try my own herbal medicines first. I'll make some tonight. We've always said the gipsy cures are best.'

Marenka mixes a calming herbal drink and goes to bed. But she does not sleep well. That night she has a very bad dream.

In her dream, Marenka sees Paul's bright red sports car. The car has an open roof. Paul is driving very fast indeed. Julia is sitting beside him and the wind is blowing her long blond hair about. The road is narrow and it is high up, on a cliff. Far below the road, far below the edge of the cliff, is the sea. Julia is calling out to Paul. 'Drive slowly! Please drive slowly!' but he only laughs. Then a look of alarm comes across Paul's face. Suddenly the car begins to go towards the edge of the cliff. Paul tries to pull the steering-wheel round, but he can't. The car is out of control. Paul's face is white. Julia screams, 'Stop! Stop!' in fear. Then, in her dream, Marenka sees the car go over the edge of the cliff, falling down, down, into the sea. Then everything goes black.

Marenka wakes up. As she wakes, she hears the voice again, saying, 'Death! Death! Death!'

'Am I going mad?' she asks herself. 'I feel very tired and anxious. Perhaps Michael is right. Perhaps I'd better see a doctor. My herbal drink didn't help me to sleep well last night.'

Chapter 9

It is Thursday morning, but Marenka does not go to the fairground. She cannot forget her dream. Instead, she goes to Julia's house. What can she do there? She doesn't clearly know, but she waits and waits.

At last, Julia comes out. Marenka follows her to the shops and then she follows her to her college. At the college gates she tries to speak to Julia, but Julia remembers her father's words at dinner-time last night – the gipsies smile at you, but bring you bad luck, not good. Julia feels afraid and walks quickly into the college, away from Marenka. She is a very nervous girl.

'I must save her! I must save her!' Marenka says to herself under her breath. Marenka does not realise that the people in the street are looking at her and thinking, 'Why is that crazy gipsy woman talking to herself?'

Marenka waits for two hours outside the college. She hopes that Julia will come out with some friends and then she can warn Julia's friends. She wants to warn Julia, but she doesn't want to frighten her.

But nobody comes out. Marenka goes home, but in the evening, she goes back to Julia's house. She waits outside it for another hour and then Paul arrives in his car. The roof is open. When Marenka sees Paul in the red sports car with the open roof, she remembers her dream again.

Then suddenly Marenka remembers something else.

'Paul is going to take Julia to the seaside on Saturday!'

she says to herself. 'He is taking her to Whitecliff Sands! It's a very pretty place, but the cliffs are very high. Perhaps he will have an accident and drive the car over the cliff. Is that the meaning of my dream? Is that the meaning of the Death card? Oh, what can I do? How can I stop them?'

Marenka looks at Paul again. He is still sitting in the car. He sees Marenka, but he does not say anything. He is impatiently waiting for Julia. He sounds the horn and she comes out of the house and gets into the car. Paul drives off very quickly, so Marenka cannot get a taxi and follow them. Marenka can only write down the number of Paul's car: H 486 DGO.

'At least I have the number of Paul's car!' she says to herself. 'If I see Paul's car parked in town, I can wait for him, and warn him not to take Julia to Whitecliff Sands.'

Marenka returns to the gipsy wagon, feeling tired and ill. Her brother is already home. Marenka tells him about her day. She wants to lay out the tarot cards again, but tonight she wants to be extra sure of the future, so she decides to lay out ten tarot cards, and not six. But the ninth card is upside-down.

'The card of the Magician!' exclaims Marenka. 'But the card is upside-down! This changes the meaning again.'

The magician in the picture is standing behind a table. In one hand, he is holding a magic wand. He is pointing up to the stars. There are also stars and moons on the magician's coat.

'The card of the Magician usually means that the gipsy magic is true,' says Marenka to Michael.

'But the card is upside-down!' exclaims Michael. 'What does that mean?'

'When the card is upside-down, it has the opposite meaning,' Marenka tells him. 'It means that science will give me the true answer, and not gipsy magic.'

'Science! Not magic!' exclaims her brother.

'Yes, Michael. When the card of the Magician is upside-down, it doesn't mean the Magician at all. It means the doctor.'

'Well, you'd better take my advice and see the doctor tomorrow, then, Marenka.'

'Yes, Michael. The cards are telling me to take your advice. I'll see Dr Jones tomorrow.'

'Well,' said Michael. 'What is the tenth card?'

Marenka puts the tenth card on the table. Again it is the Death card, the smiling skeleton, but this time, Marenka smiles too.

'The Death card,' she says. 'But because the Death card is next to the doctor, there is no need to worry. The doctor saves people from death. I shall not need to lay out the tarot cards again.'

Chapter 10

The next morning is Friday and Marenka goes to the doctor's early. She tells Dr Jones everything about Julia and Paul. She also tells him about the voice inside her head, saying 'Death! Death! Death!' and about the skull in the crystal ball. Dr Jones listens very carefully. She was expecting him to laugh, but he does not laugh at her at all. When she finishes her story, he gives her some tablets.

'This is a very interesting story,' he says. 'These tablets will help you to relax. You'd better come and see me again next week. Perhaps you will need to go into hospital for a few days' rest. I'll call Dr Mitchell about your case now.'

Marenka is very alarmed to hear this. She does not want to go into hospital. She wants to save Julia's life! She takes the tablets and leaves. As she goes out of the door, she sees Dr Jones pick up the telephone. For the first time in her life, Marenka puts her ear to the door and listens. She hears Dr Jones' voice.

'Get me the Dickinson Psychiatric Hospital, please,' he says to his receptionist. 'Extension 218.'

'The Dickinson Psychiatric Hospital!' exclaims Marenka to herself. 'Why, he thinks I'm crazy!'

'Oh, is that Dr Mitchell?' she hears Dr Jones continue into the telephone. 'I have a case here that perhaps will interest you . . . a gipsy woman . . . She came to see me today . . . Yes, she hears voices . . . She talks all the time about a young couple . . . Yes, this couple is soon getting

married . . . She has a crazy belief that the young woman is going to die . . . No, no . . . She can't get this idea out of her head . . . Strange behaviour? Yes, she follows the young woman about everywhere . . . Violent? No, I don't think this gipsy woman is violent, but she talks about death a lot . . . She seems to talk to herself . . . No, she hasn't got a fixed address . . . Yes, she seems to think that all the world is against her because she is a gipsy . . . Envious? Perhaps she is envious of the couple's money and success. Yet she seems to think that she is better than everyone else because she is a true gipsy . . . Would you see her next week? I think she will need to stay in hospital . . . Thank you so much. Goodbye.'

Marenka listens in horror. Is Dr Jones really talking about her? Surely it's not possible. He simply thinks she is crazy? He did not understand! She will certainly not go back again next week!

Marenka leaves the doctor's and goes outside into the street. She catches the bus and looks sadly out of the window. 'How can I help Julia?' she is wondering. The bus goes through the centre of town. Suddenly she sees a bright red sports car. It is parked outside a tall, smart office block. Marenka takes a good look at the car – yes, it *is* Paul's car, H 486 DGO.

'Paul probably works in that office block,' she says to herself. 'I wonder what his job is.'

Then, as she looks at the car, she hears the voice again inside her head, saying strongly, 'Death! Death! Death!'

'I must warn him not to take Julia to Whitecliff Sands in that car,' thinks Marenka. 'If Paul works in that office block, he will leave at five o'clock. I'll go back at five o'clock and try to warn him. He mustn't take Julia to the seaside tomorrow – I must stop him.'

It is now lunch-time, so Marenka goes back to the gipsy wagon. She takes one of her tablets and she makes some tea with herbs. She begins to feel calmer. She lies down on the bed. She has the same dream of the red sports car and she sees it going over the cliff again. Then everything goes black, just as before. But this time, Marenka falls into a very deep sleep. When she wakes, it is late afternoon. She feels much better, but she again hears the voice inside her head, more strongly than ever, saying, 'Death! Death! Death!' In her mind, she again sees the picture of the skull with the long hair down to the shoulders. Her dream is still fresh in her mind, too.

'What's the time?' she says to herself, as she looks at her watch. 'Oh no, it's a quarter past four already! I must be at Paul's office by five o'clock. I must hurry! I must stop their trip to the seaside tomorrow.'

Marenka starts to walk to Paul's office. It is getting late, but she is nearly there. Everyone is leaving work. All the cars are moving fast because it is Friday afternoon and everyone wants to get home quickly. Marenka looks at her watch again. She must cross the street and go round the next corner before she gets to the office block.

'Perhaps I'll just catch him as he leaves the office,' Marenka thinks. So she starts to run.

'I hope he will listen to me. He is impatient just like Julia's father,' she thinks anxiously. 'I must get there in time,' she repeats to herself as she runs. People look at her hard, but she cannot think of anything except saving Julia. She hurries across the busy road without looking at the cars.

Suddenly a bright red sports car comes round the corner. It is going very fast indeed. Marenka turns. She is very surprised and so she does not move out of the way quickly. She only looks in horror at the car. She sees Paul's alarmed, white face as he tries to pull the steering-wheel in another direction. It is just like his face in her dream. Marenka also sees the pretty face of Julia, sitting next to Paul in the car.

Marenka hears Julia scream 'Stop! Stop!' in fear, just as she did in her dream. She also hears the noise of the brakes as Paul tries to stop the car suddenly. Then Marenka feels a burning pain in her side.

Marenka falls to the ground. The car has hit her. As she falls, her bright red gipsy scarf falls off her head. Without her scarf now, her long black hair falls over her shoulders, like the hair of the skull in the crystal ball. Her face is as white as the skull in the crystal too. As she falls, Marenka hears the words 'Death! Death! Death!' ring strongly inside her head for the last time.

Marenka is lying on the ground. Paul and Julia jump out of the car. Marenka hears the car doors as they slam shut. Then she hears Julia's voice, saying nervously,

'Why, it's the poor, mad gipsy woman from the fairground. The one who followed me everywhere yesterday! We've killed her.'

'No,' answers Paul. '*We* didn't kill her – she killed herself. She deliberately threw herself in front of my car.

She wanted to die. She was mad, completely mad.'

'I am the Fool,' thinks Marenka. 'I am Fortune's Fool. That Death card was for me.'

Then everything goes black.

The tenth tarot card is always for the questioner.

Glossary

a bag of nerves   a very nervous person
to beg   to ask for money in the streets
client   customer
cloudy   not clear
crazy   mad, out of your mind
fairground   a place with lots of entertainments, games, etc.
flashy   too extravagant and colourful
for a joke   not with serious intentions
gipsy wagon   the travelling cart that travelling people (gipsies) lived in
grave   tomb
it's worth it   the cost is all right
jolly   happy
to lie   to say something that is not true
neigh   the sound a horse makes
to quarrel   to fight, have angry discussions
reckless   behaving dangerously
rubbish   nonsense
to sip   to drink slowly
skull   a head with no eyes or skin
a stroke of luck   a fortunate thing to happen
white heather   a plant which gipsies sometimes sell to bring good luck